Chocolate Milk with a Side of Beauty

BY: TIFFANY CASH-HARRIS

Chocolate Milk With A Side Of Beauty

Paperback ISBN: 978-1-7375096-0-8
Hardcover ISBN: 978-1-7375096-1-5

10 9 8 7 6 5 4 3 2 1
Printed in the United States

Priceless Publishing®
Coral Springs, Fl
www.pricelesspublishing.co

DEDICATION

I dedicate this book to the little girl that still lives inside of me.
And to every brown and black little girl learning to love themselves.

GABRIELLE is a little girl with dark brown skin like a tall glass of chocolate milk. Her **MOMMY** says that her black skin makes her as sweet as a chocolate chip cookie. Her **DADDY** says that her black skin makes her the prettiest girl in the whole world.

GABRIELLE has two best friends named **BROOKE** and **KALYCE**. They have beautiful black skin just like Gabrielle. They love having sleepovers, playing Mommy and Baby, and playing dress-up in the mirror. As Brooke and Kalyce smiled at their reflections in the mirror, Gabrielle had a frown on her face.

"Look at us!" shouted **BROOKE**.
"We look so pretty!" said **KALYCE**.

"I don't think I look pretty." said GABRIELLE

"Your skin is the color of vanilla ice cream." said GABRIELLE to BROOKE.

"Your skin is the color of caramel." said GABRIELLE to KALYCE.

"But my skin is the color of a tall glass of chocolate milk." said GABRIELLE.

The next day **GABRIELLE** goes to school and sees her teacher, Ms. Harris. Gabrielle sees that **MS. HARRIS'S** skin is tan like honey, and not dark brown like a tall glass of chocolate milk. Gabrielle starts to imagine herself with Ms. Harris's skin.

She whispers to herself, ***"I like her skin better than mine. I want MS. HARRIS' S skin. My skin is too ugly."***

The school bell rings and **GABRIELLE** snaps out of it. She hurries to pack her stuff up and

Her **DAD** sees her and says, *"Gabby, I have a big surprise for you at home."*

GABRIELLE says,

Is it a new **DOLL**?
Is it a great, big bowl of **ICE-CREAM**?
Is it a brand-new **DRESS**?
Is it a tube of new **LIPGLOSS**?

"Daddy, Daddy, what is it!" said **GABRIELLE**.

When they got home, **DADDY** told Gabrielle to cover her eyes. **GABRIELLE** could not stop giggling. She was so excited! After she covers her eyes, Daddy starts to count backwards,

"5...4...3...2...1! You can open your eyes now!" shouted **DADDY**.

"It's a cookie party!" **GABRIELLE** said with excitement.

She gave her **DADDY** a great big hug and shouted, ***"Thank you so much. I love my surprise!"***

All her favorite cookies were there! Sugar cookies, peanut butter cookies, and even chocolate chip cookies.

"You can have two cookies to eat before dinner," said **DADDY**.

"Thank you sooo much for the cookies," said **GABRIELLE**.

"You're welcome! I am so happy to have such a pretty girl to eat cookies with," says **DADDY**.

"I like eating cookies with you too, Daddy, but I don't think I am a pretty girl," said **GABRIELLE**.

"Why do you think that, Gabby?" Daddy asked.

"My skin is so dark. I don't like my black skin. I want prettier skin like **BROOKE**, **KALYCE** *or even* **MS. HARRIS**,*"* Gabrielle said.

Gabrielle's Daddy picked her up and gave her a great big hug. He took her in front of the mirror and said, ***"Gabby, let me show you something. Brooke, Kalyce and Ms. Harris have black skin just like you. But*** **BLACK PEOPLE** ***are like*** **MAGIC** ***— we have different skin colors. Your skin is perfect. It is a beautiful dark brown that's as smooth as hot cocoa on a cold winter day."***

"You really think so, Daddy?" *asked* **GABRIELLE**.

"Yes, I do think so!" said Daddy.

"As a matter of fact, your skin is beautiful like SHURI and NAKIA from BLACK PANTHER, and it glows just like PRINCESS TIANA'S!

"Your skin shines bright in the SUNLIGHT and blends in perfectly with the MOONLIGHT.

Your skin is just like my favorite drink — a tall glass of CHOCOLATE MILK, BUT WITH A SIDE OF BEAUTY."

***"Aawww thank you,* DADDY!"** Gabrielle shouted with a big smile on her face.

"I get it now black skin comes in many colors but we are all beautiful. I will always love my beautiful chocolate-milk skin," *said Gabrielle.*

Handing her a glass of chocolate milk, Daddy asked, ***"Do you promise?"***

Smiling, **GABRIELLE** replied, ***"I promise."***

MY NAME IS

AND I PROMISE TO ALWAYS LOVE MY SKIN.

ABOUT THE AUTHOR

TIFFANY CASH-HARRIS is a wife, mother, and educator. As a child, Tiffany silently struggled with her shade of blackness which led into adulthood. After overcoming this insecurity, learning to truly love her shade of blackness has influenced Tiffany to write **CHOCOLATE MILK WITH A SIDE OF BEAUTY**. She wrote this book intending to change the colorist mindset that young black girls tend to follow.

JOIN THE CONVERSATION

Follow the author on Instagram

@tiffanycashharris

Email **tiffanycashharris@gmail.com**

To place a bulk order for this book

Have this book added to school's curriculum

Book the author for an event

CPSIA information can be obtained
at www.ICGtesting.com
Printed in the USA
BVHW021315260721
612869BV00007B/500
9781737509615